Helping America Read

by Karen Bornemann Spies

Maxwell Macmillan Canada
Toronto

Maxwell Macmillan International
New York Oxford Singapore Sydney

Photographic Acknowledgments

The photographs are reproduced through the courtesy of: The White House; Carol T. Powers, the White House; Ashley Hall; Susan Biddle, the White House; David Valdez, the White House; University of Texas of the Permian Basin, Odessa, Texas.

Library of Congress Cataloging-in-Publication Data

Spies, Karen Bornemann.
Barbara Bush : Helping America Read / by Karen Bornemann Spies.
p. cm. — (Taking part)
Summary: A biography of Barbara Bush, whose down-to-earth manner has made her one of the most popular First Ladies ever.
ISBN 0-87518-488-X
1. Bush, Barbara, 1925- —Juvenile literature. 2. Bush, George, 1924- —Juvenile literature. 3. Presidents—United States—Wives-Biography—Juvenile literature. [1. Bush, Barbara, 1925- 2. First ladies.] I. Title.
E883.B87S65 1991
973.928′092—dc20 91-17725
[B]

Dillon Press
Macmillan Publishing Company
866 Third Avenue
New York, NY 10022

Maxwell Macmillan Canada, Inc.
1200 Eglinton Avenue East
Suite 200
Don Mills, Ontario M3C 3N1

Macmillan Publishing Company is part of the Maxwell Communication Group of Companies.

First edition
Printed in the United States of America
10 9 8 7 6 5 4 3 2 1

Contents

Introduction

On January 20, 1989, Barbara Bush stood beside her husband as he was sworn in as the forty-first president of the United States. At that moment, she became the first lady of the country, a job for which she was well prepared.

Barbara met many government leaders during the time George Bush served as United States ambassador to the United Nations and envoy to China. During the eight years her husband was vice president, Barbara led the Ladies of the Senate. Bar, as her husband calls her, was excited about living and working in the White House.

Barbara Bush has spent forty-six years of married life supporting her husband in his path to the presidency. Together they have lived in seventeen different cities and raised five children. While George Bush worked in the oil business and later built a career in politics, Barbara kept the family ties strong. She served as a Cub Scout den mother, carpool driver, and Sunday school teacher. "Everyone always wanted to come over to our house," said her son Marvin.

Her love of family grew from the values she learned in childhood. She was very close to her father, Marvin Pierce, chairman of the McCall Corporation, which published *McCall's* magazine. Her mother, Pauline, raised the four Pierce children to show consideration for others. "We were brought up to look after people's feelings," Barbara recalls.

Helping others has long been an important part of her life. When her daughter Robin died of leukemia, Barbara began visiting children who had cancer. She also started a hospital thrift shop to raise money for sick children.

Her main project as first lady is helping adults and children learn to read. In 1989 she started the Barbara Bush Foundation for Family Literacy. The foundation raises money to support reading programs throughout the United States. She has also written two books. The profit from their sales is used to train reading teachers and to give books to children who cannot afford to buy them.

Barbara Bush loves her life as the first lady. Her friendly, outgoing nature has made her very popular, at times even more popular than her husband. Barbara Bush has reached her own time to be famous.

These two young cousins enjoy listening as their grandmother reads a storybook. Their grandmother is Barbara Bush, first lady of the United States.

Rye Times

A group of children sit at the feet of their smiling, white-haired grandmother. In her lap, she holds a brown-spotted spaniel and a book. She begins to read. When the children laugh at the funny parts of the story, she laughs, too. Who is this woman? She is Barbara Pierce Bush, wife of the forty-first president of the United States.

Barbara Bush is more than a friendly looking grandmother with beautiful white hair. One of her friends said she is "a combination of gentleness and steel." She does not apologize for her many strong opinions. One thing that makes her angry is criticism of her husband. Barbara has devoted her life to supporting him and their family.

She has not chosen to seek fame herself. Yet her quick wit and friendly personality have made her one of America's most popular first ladies.

Barbara Pierce was born on June 8, 1925, in New York City. She was the third child of Marvin and Pauline Robinson Pierce. The Pierces lived in Rye, New York, a town near the Connecticut border, about one hour away from New York City.

Barbara's father worked his way up the company ladder to become the chairman of the McCall Corporation. This company published magazines such as *Redbook* and *McCall's*. Like most women of the time, Barbara's mother worked at home, taking care of their four children, Martha, Jimmy, Barbara, and Scott.

The Pierce children were raised to have a strong sense of loyalty to their family. Marvin Pierce saved all the letters his children wrote to him and kept a diary of what they did. He believed parents should help their children receive a fine education, set a good example, and give them all the love they could. From her mother, Barbara learned to love both animals and gardening. Mrs. Pierce was known to keep injured squirrels in the bathtub until they healed, and often fixed birds' broken wings. She enjoyed working in her garden and was in charge of conservation for the Garden Clubs of America.

Barbara believes her mother made the world a more beautiful place. Mrs. Pierce filled their home with antique china, crystal, and furniture. She did lovely needlepoint, a kind of skilled needlework which Barbara learned as an adult.

But in many ways, Mrs. Pierce was not easy to live with. She spent hours at the hospital with Scott, her youngest son. He underwent seven years of treatment for a cyst, which Mrs. Pierce called a "bad place" in the bone marrow of his shoulder. Mrs. Pierce was gone so much and was so worried about Scott that it was hard for Barbara to have a good relationship with her. Barbara, who was seven when Scott's treatment began, said that she couldn't understand the strain her mother suffered. Now, as a mother and grandmother, she can.

Barbara learned to look at life in a different way than her mother. Pauline Pierce couldn't enjoy each moment to the fullest because she spent too much time hoping the next day would be better. Barbara appreciates her life the way it is. One of her favorite expressions is "Life is right now." She believes in enjoying herself during the good times and making the best of difficult times.

Because she didn't receive much attention from her mother, Barbara turned to her father. He had a teasing sense of humor, which Barbara inherited from him. She is known for her quick wit, but she is careful to tease only people who know her well.

Barbara's father was an excellent athlete, who encouraged his daughter's interest in tennis, swimming, and climbing trees. When he was at Miami University, Marvin Pierce was a pitcher on the baseball team, captain of the football team, and a winning tennis player.

Growing up in Rye, New York, Barbara lived with her family in a three-story, five-bedroom brick home. Big trees surrounded the house, and an artificial pond was nearby. There were many things to do in her neighborhood, which was known as Indian Village. Favorite activities were riding bikes and cutting out paper dolls. She played imagination games with several friends, acting out dog stories and books such as Louisa May Alcott's *Little Women*.

With her friends, she took tennis and swimming

Seven-year-old Barbara.

lessons at the private Manursing Island Club on Long Island Sound in New York. Friday nights they learned dancing and etiquette at Miss Covington's Dancing School. Barbara often danced the boy's part because she was already five feet eight inches tall at the age of twelve.

She loved dogs. First the family had Scotties. Later they had cairn terriers, including Barbara's own, which was named Sandy. When her mother's dog had puppies, they were kept in her parents' bathroom upstairs. Mr. Pierce worried about stepping on the puppies in the middle of the night, so he was always glad when they grew too big to stay in the bathroom.

Barbara began school in 1931 when she was six. On the first day, her mother held her hand and took her to meet the teacher. Then she left without saying good-bye. At first, Barbara said she felt abandoned. But she liked school so much that she forgave her mother by the end of the day.

In seventh grade, Barbara enrolled in the private Rye Country Day School. She stayed there until her junior year in high school, when she left to attend Ashley Hall in Charleston, South Carolina. Ashley Hall was a boarding school, where students lived in

Barbara (far left) *plays the role of Beatrice in an Ashley Hall production of* Much Ado about Nothing *in 1942.*

dormitories instead of at home. Barbara had to take an overnight train to get to the school. She remembers feeling very lonely as she walked up the flight of stairs to the third floor. But she says that her loneliness lasted "for about four minutes," until she got to know some of the other girls.

She enjoyed acting in plays at Ashley Hall. Barbara also held the school records for speed-knitting and for underwater swimming. She swam two and one-half times across the pool in one breath. To this day, she enjoys swimming.

In December 1941, the students of Ashley Hall learned about the Japanese bombing of Pearl Harbor, which forced America's entry into World War II. Headmistress Mary Vardrine McBee announced the terrible news when the drama club was rehearsing its annual Christmas pageant. Most of the girls called home to make sure their families were all right.

Several days later, Barbara went home for the Christmas holidays. There she met a boy who would make the war a very real part of her life.

ASHLEY HALL Newsletter

"Academic Excellence for Four Generations"

WINTER 1980

172 Rutledge Avenue, Charleston, South Carolina 29403

A CONVERSATION WITH BARBARA BUSH

Some weeks before the Presidential election on November 5, we contacted Mrs. George Bush **(Barbara Pierce '43)** by letter requesting a telephone interview for our Winter Newsletter. We knew our readers would be interested in her reactions to the past year's activities and to the results of the election. We were granted permission to do the interview and then learned that Ambassador and Mrs. Bush would be in Charleston on November 1 for a Republican Fundraising Breakfast. We were able to arrange a personal meeting with Mrs. Bush and spent a delightful half-hour talking with her. On Thursday after Tuesday's election, Mrs. Bush called us from Los Angeles where she and her husband were visiting with President-elect and Mrs. Reagan. The interview which follows is a transcription of that telephone call. WCSC Radio graciously taped the interview for Ashley Hall and in return had the opportunity to further question Mrs. Bush. — *The Editors*

DEE DEE: "So you say your life has changed, Mrs. Bush."

MRS. BUSH: "Well, only because we won and quickly got on an airplane and flew out to be with the Reagans for lunch yesterday and some talk, and today George has a press conference. Then we are going to fly back to Houston, Texas, tonight — and I think after the week-end we are going to try to go off for a little rest."

DEE DEE: "I am sure you can well use it. I know it has been very exciting for you. Now, I know you have traveled all about the country, and having seen the United States and the grass roots of this country, so to speak, what do you perceive to be the real mood of the majority of the country? Are you encouraged or discouraged?"

MRS. BUSH: "We never thought the country was sick at all, we always thought there was a great lack of leadership, and of course the mood of the country really is one of wanting to get inflation under control, and I think the people were a little bit frightened because they did not see us going in a direction that was going to solve the problem of the economy. The country is good, the people are fantastic! And I really think the big surprise of the election was, No. 1, the mandate that Governor Reagan got; No. 2 was the terrific turnover in the Senate, the first time, I think since 1956 that the control of the Senate has changed parties. That will make a tremendous difference because it means that the staff will change, and that is very important."

DEE DEE: "That's wonderful. I think that will be supportive for your policies and whatever it is that you, as a group, decide to do. Do you feel, then, that your contact with the people, and the mood, and certainly the mandate of the country in the victory has influenced or changed in any way your perception of what must be done by the Reagan-Bush White House?"

MRS. BUSH: "No, because you know Governor Reagan ran a big State, and I think he knows that jobs are very, very important, and I don't think it has changed our perception really — the problems that were there are there today, and more so — inner-city problems, lack of jobs, lack of incentive in business, in . . . . oh just lack of incentive has been very obvious to us from the beginning. I hope we can change all that."

DEE DEE: "Was there anything you found surprising as you traveled about the country, that was unexpected and surprising to the good or to the bad?"

MRS. BUSH: "No, I wasn't surprised because George and I have moved twenty-seven times since we have been married, but I am always sort of overwhelmed by the goodness of people — always — generosity, lovingness — I was not surprised at all by that."

DEE DEE: "To what do you attribute your obvious self-confidence, and certain ability, and willingness to travel the campaign trail across the country?"

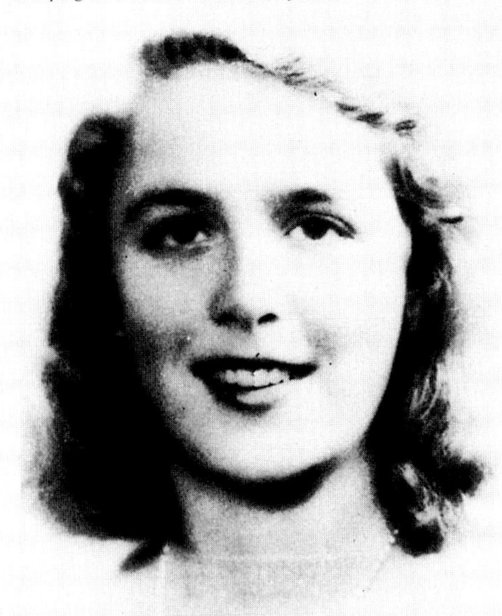

Barbara Pierce Bush - 1943
(Courtesy of the Charleston News & Courier)

Poppy Bush

Barbara wore a red-and-green Christmas dress to the country club dance. The dress brought out the glow of her naturally wavy, reddish brown hair. As she danced, a tall slender boy watched her. He noticed her lively smile and laughing eyes. He knew he wanted to get to know her, so he asked his friend Jack Wozencroft to introduce them.

The young man was George Bush, nicknamed Poppy after his grandfather. He asked Barbara to dance, but just then the orchestra began to play a waltz. Poppy didn't waltz, so they sat out that dance and several others.

As they talked, they began to fall in love. Barbara was only sixteen, George just seventeen. But they

A 1980 Ashley Hall newsletter printed a photograph of Barbara as she appeared in 1943.

knew that their romance was something special. Barbara said she could hardly breathe when George was in the room. Poppy admired many qualities that he saw in Barbara. She was a person who was very sure of herself. She was also ready to reach out to others and didn't seem to worry about what people thought of her.

After the Christmas holidays, Barbara went back to Ashley Hall and George returned to Andover, Massachusetts, where he went to prep school. Barbara talked so much about Poppy Bush that her roommates knew she cared about him deeply. When she wasn't studying, she knitted socks for Poppy or wrote him letters. He wrote many letters back to her, and she read aloud the newsy parts to her roommates. Sadly, the grown-up Barbara admits, she didn't save these letters.

That summer, George invited Barbara to visit his

Barbara and George before they were married, with George's youngest brother, Bucky.

family at their vacation home in Kennebunkport, Maine. They became engaged to be married, but didn't announce it publicly until the fall of 1943. By this time, George had joined the navy. When he finished flight training, he was assigned to a torpedo-bomber squadron aboard the aircraft carrier *San Jacinto*. He named his plane *Barbara*.

While George was flying missions against the Japanese in the Pacific, Barbara enrolled at Smith College. She was the captain of the soccer team and enjoyed spending time with her college friends. But she admits that she wasn't a very good student because she spent too much time thinking about George.

During her sophomore year in college, Barbara, like many young women at that time, dropped out of school to plan her wedding. She did not know that George had been shot down during a bombing mission in September. She learned about it three or four days after George sent word to his family that he was safe. Later she said she was glad she hadn't known sooner, since she would have been worried.

George arrived home on Christmas Eve, 1944. What a joyous time of tears, hugs, and laughter! He and Barbara were married on January 6, 1945, in the

Rye Presbyterian Church, during George's short leave. Nineteen-year-old Barbara stood five feet ten inches tall in her satin gown and the veil that George's mother had worn in her own wedding. George was handsome and slim in his navy dress blues. Barbara said later, "I married the first man I ever kissed."

They spent their honeymoon on Sea Island, Georgia. Then the navy assigned twenty-year-old George Bush to train new pilots. The Bushes moved to the Naval Air Station at Norfolk, Virginia, where they shared a nearby house with three other couples.

On the night of August 14, 1945, Barbara and George were with friends at the officers' club when they heard President Truman's announcement: The war was over! After joining the celebration, Barbara and George went to a nearby church to give thanks for the war's end and to remember all those who had died during the battles.

Now that the war was over, the Bushes, like so many other young couples at that time, were ready to move on with their lives. George enrolled at Yale University, where he studied economics and held many leadership positions on campus. George was captain of the baseball team, and Barbara, who loved baseball, was the official scorekeeper.

The Bushes lived in an old house that had been divided into thirteen tiny apartments for returning servicemen and their families. They were very careful with their money, especially after the birth of their first child, George Walker Bush, on July 6, 1946.

George graduated in June 1948. He was offered a job in his father's banking firm, but he turned it down. He and Barbara talked about starting out on their own, without any help from their families. George said that he wanted to seek his fortune in the oil business in Texas. At first Barbara was not sure

George and Barbara's wedding day.

Odessa, Texas, in 1950.

she wanted to leave the East, where both their families lived. But then Barbara did what she has continued to do throughout her married life—she supported her husband. The Bushes took their savings of three thousand dollars and moved to Odessa, Texas.

Odessa was a small town in West Texas on the

edge of the oil fields. The Bushes lived in half of a tiny house on Seventh Street. It had a small kitchen, one bedroom, and one bathroom, which they shared with their neighbors.

George earned just over three hundred dollars a month sweeping out warehouses and painting oil-drilling machinery. In 1949 he was promoted to a better job selling drilling tools, and the company sent him to California. There the Bushes' second child, a daughter named Robin, was born in December. The family lived in five different cities during the year that George worked in California. George traveled about a thousand miles a week, while Barbara stayed home to care for young George and Robin.

Lively little Robin was named after Barbara's mother, Pauline Robinson Pierce. Mrs. Pierce had been killed in an automobile accident two months before Robin was born. Barbara's father convinced her that she should not come to New York for the funeral because her baby was due soon. Mr. Pierce worried that the trip would be too hard on Barbara. Looking back Barbara now wishes that she had gone.

Soon after Robin's birth, the Bush family moved to Midland, Texas. Midland was in the midst of an oil boom. Ambitious young families had come there from all over the United States. Barbara and George bought a home on East Maple Street in an area that became known as "Easter Egg Row." The houses were all alike, so the builder had painted them each a different bright color. The Bushes' home was light blue.

The Bushes made many close friends, such as Marion and C. Fred Chambers. The two families, like most young families in Midland, did not have any relatives in town, since they had moved there from somewhere else in the country. So the Bushes often invited the Chamberses and other families over on Sunday afternoons for hamburgers.

In 1951 George Bush formed his own oil company with his neighbor John Overbey. He traveled all over the world, searching for oil. But Barbara had to stay home, because they couldn't afford for her to go along.

Moving away from their families changed Barbara's and George's lives. She feels that the move was good for their marriage. It helped them both grow up quickly and learn to depend on each other. They soon needed each other's support, especially when their daughter Robin became seriously ill.

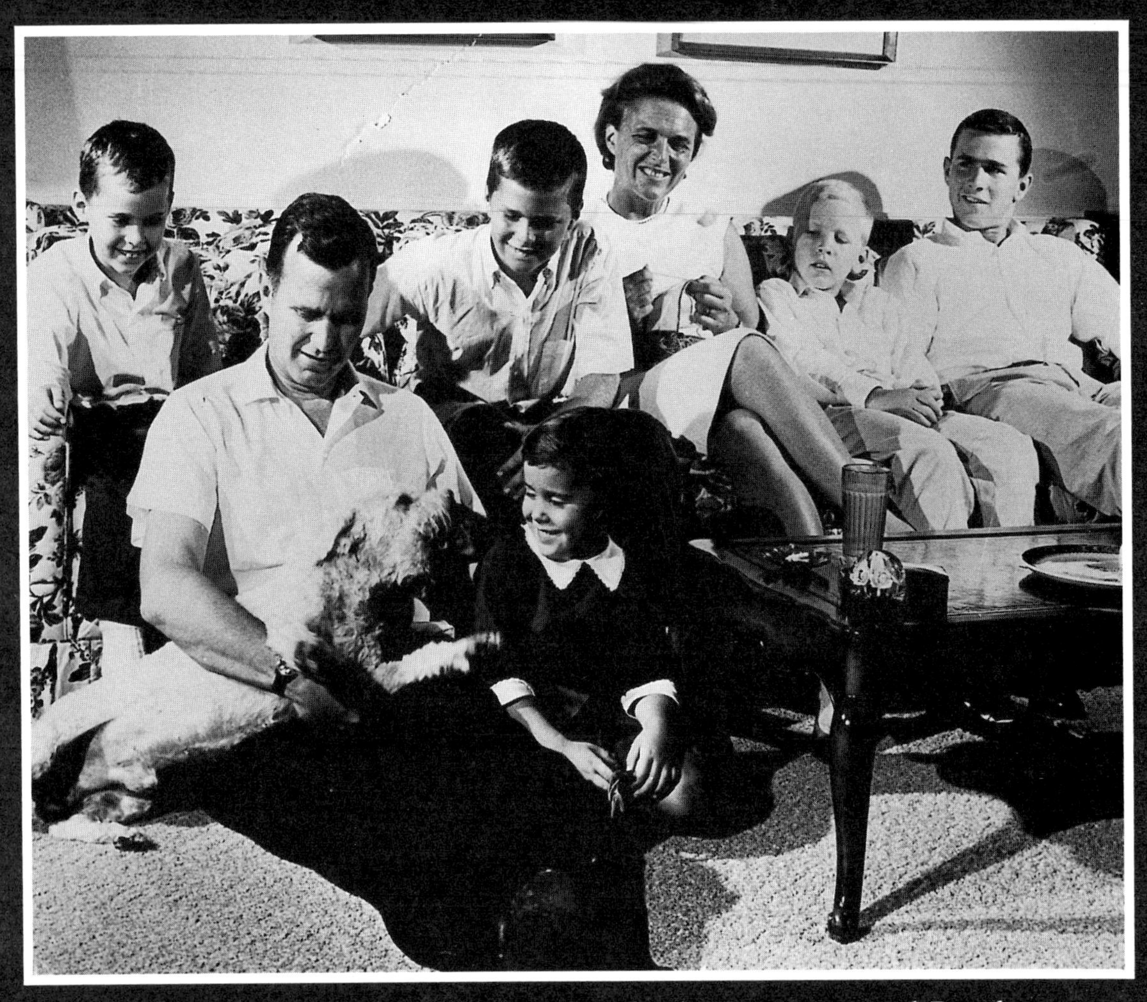

The Bush family in 1964. Seated on the floor are George and Dorothy. Seated on the sofa (from left to right) *are Marvin, Jeb, Barbara, Neil, and George Walker.*

Sadness and Joy

On a spring morning in 1953, three-year-old Robin Bush woke up feeling too tired to play. This was not the way Robin usually acted. She looked normal, but Barbara took her in to the doctor for tests. When the test results came back, the Bushes found out that Robin had leukemia, a cancer of the blood. The doctor said she might live only a few more weeks.

Barbara and George were stunned. They decided they could not sit back and wait for their daughter to die. They called George's uncle, Dr. John Walker, who was a specialist in treating cancer. Uncle John asked them to bring Robin to Memorial Hospital in New York City. The doctors there were doing important research on fighting leukemia.

During the next six months, Barbara spent many hours with Robin in the hospital. Barbara's hair began to turn white from the stress. On weekends, George flew back and forth between Texas and New York. George and Barbara encouraged each other and prayed, but the doctors couldn't save Robin. She was three years and ten months old when she died.

When Robin was ill, Barbara never cried, although George did. Now that Robin was gone, Barbara felt she couldn't stop crying. George held her in his arms and let her weep. They helped each other and received strength from their faith in God.

Robin's death brought Barbara and George closer together. They would never get over her death, but their other children helped ease the pain. John Ellis ("Jeb") was born in 1953, Neil Mallon in 1955, Marvin Pierce in 1956, and Dorothy Walker ("Doro") in 1959.

By the time Doro was born, the Bushes lived in Houston on Briar Drive. It was a wonderful home for a large family, with a big playroom and a backyard swimming pool. The yard was perfect for hosting family barbecues like the ones the Bushes had held in Midland.

Barbara managed the household so that it ran smoothly. Jeb said he never understood how his mother kept track of the five children's schedules. Her home was so spotless that friend Marion Chambers said: "She always made me feel like a slob."

In addition to teaching Sunday school, Barbara was involved in charity activities, such as running a hospital thrift shop. She started the shop the year after Robin's death. To help ease the pain, she kept busy visiting poor neighborhoods to tell people about the shop. She also called on wealthy friends to get them to contribute money.

Still, it often seemed to Barbara as if she spent her life in car pools and watched hundreds of hours of Little League games. Sometimes she experienced what she called "bumpy moments," when she felt jealous of her husband and his world travels.

Even so, Barbara made the neighborhood children welcome. They often used the Bush home as their meeting place. But still the Bush children had to follow strict rules. They were not allowed to pick on others or hurt their feelings.

The Bush children were encouraged to step out on their own. Barbara and George did not want their children to stay in the shadow of their successful father. Jeb, Neil, and Marvin started a weekly neighborhood newspaper. All the children were encouraged to do well in school and become involved in sports.

After living several years in Houston, George

decided that he wanted to start a new career in public service. His decision was not surprising, since his father, Prescott Bush, Sr., had been a United States senator between 1952 and 1963. The elder Mr. Bush went into politics after he had made his mark as a successful banker in New York City.

George, like his father, had become a success in business. He and Barbara had a nice home and had saved enough money to send their children to college. But they both believed that the more advantages a person had, the more he or she should help others.

George's first political race was for chairmanship of the Harris County Republican party. Barbara went with him night after night as he met with groups of voters. To keep herself awake while she listened to the same speech she had already heard 150 times, Barbara learned to do needlepoint. George won the election and worked hard to build party membership.

Barbara found that she loved campaigning, and she worked hard to support her husband. In 1964 George ran for the United States Senate. Barbara went door-to-door, calling on voters. Her name tag said "Barbara," without the "Bush." She was afraid if voters knew who she was, they wouldn't give her their honest opinion of her husband. Unfortunately, George lost in a close election.

Two years later, he decided to run for the U.S. Congress, to represent Texas's Seventh District, which includes Houston. Barbara sent a letter to the 73,000 women voters in the district. She told them about George's sense of humor, fairness, and faith in God.

Her friendly manner helped him win votes. She was good at remembering people's names, but shy about speaking in front of groups. Barbara practiced many hours and overcame her fears. Today audiences

George and Barbara in Houston, Texas, on victory night of the congressional campaign in 1966.

sense her strength, ideas, and personal warmth whenever she speaks.

This time George won the election, so the family moved to Washington, D.C. They eventually settled in a brick home Barbara found on a quiet cul-de-sac. Many interesting people lived on the street, including

Supreme Court Justice Potter Stewart and his wife, Andy.

Barbara was an actively involved neighbor. She mowed the grass in a circular planting area at the end of the cul-de-sac and kept a garden that was the envy of everyone on the street. She continued the Bush tradition of backyard barbecues and seemed to attract people to her like a magnet. They joked about being among Barbara's two thousand friends.

After George had served two terms in Congress, he resigned his seat to run again for the Senate. President Nixon supported his campaign with money and a campaign appearance in Texas. Again the race was close, but George was the loser. So President Nixon gave him the job of ambassador to the United Nations. The United Nations is an international organization in which nations work together to solve problems such as hunger and disease.

The family moved into the ambassador's residence in New York City, an apartment in the Waldorf Towers. Barbara and George showed their pride in America by decorating the apartment with paintings by American artists. They held many dinners and receptions in their apartment, and enjoyed taking other diplomats along on family picnics and to New York Mets games. One of the team's owners was George's uncle Herbert.

Two years later, in 1973, the Bushes moved back to Washington, D.C. President Nixon had asked George to be chairman of the Republican National Committee. Soon the president was scrambling for support. His top aides had arranged for important papers to be stolen from the Democratic National Committee's offices in the Watergate building. When it came out that Nixon had known about the burglary, George Bush told him he should resign. Nixon did,

岁
世界

and Vice President Gerald Ford took over as president.

It was now 1974. George felt disillusioned after the Watergate scandal. He wanted to work somewhere other than Washington, D.C. President Ford sent him to Beijing, the capital of the People's Republic of China. George represented the United States government as envoy, which is like an ambassador.

Barbara loved China. The children, who were nearly grown, stayed in school in the United States. Barbara had George all to herself. She studied Chinese, practiced t'ai chi, and designed a room-size needlepoint rug that represented her time in China.

Barbara and George brought along their cocker spaniel, C. Fred Bush, named after their friend C. Fred Chambers. Dogs were rare in China, because they had been killed off after the 1949 revolution to stop the spread of rabies. When Barbara took C. Fred on walks, some of the people were afraid of him.

Barbara and George riding bicycles in China in 1974.

Others called him *mao*, the Chinese word for cat. Barbara learned to say in Chinese, "Don't worry. He's only a little dog, and he doesn't bite." C. Fred often went along when Barbara rode her bicycle. She attached a long rope to his collar and rode up and down the streets with him running at her side. Because of the dirty air in Beijing, C. Fred changed from a honey-colored dog to a gray one.

After only thirteen months in China, the Bushes returned to Washington. President Ford needed George Bush to head the Central Intelligence Agency (CIA). The CIA is in charge of gathering secret information for national security.

Barbara and George left Beijing with mixed feelings. They were satisfied with the job they had done overseas but were worried about the new position. As director of the CIA, George could not go to any political functions. That meant the Bushes were left out of most Washington parties. He could not talk about his work at home, because so much of it was top secret. After being a partner in George's work in China, Barbara now felt left out. She said later that this was her least favorite of all George's occupations.

George's job change was part of the reason Barbara suffered a depression in 1976. She was often alone because George was busy with his job and their children were grown and no longer at home. Barbara said she often felt like crying.

She fought her deep feelings of sadness by throwing herself into service work. She volunteered at the Washington Home, a health-care center for seriously ill and dying people. She did simple tasks, such as washing patients' hair and changing their bed sheets.

After about six months, she no longer felt depressed. She was ready to face new challenges.

The Bush family in 1979. Top row, from left to right: *Marvin; George (age 3); Jeb; George Bush; George Walker; George Walker's wife, Laura.* Bottom row, left to right: *Jeb's wife, Columba; Noelle (age 2); Dorothy; Barbara Bush; Neil.*

Life in the White House

On May 1, 1979, George Bush announced that he was running for president of the United States. The entire Bush family worked on the election campaign, making speeches and meeting with voters. Despite their efforts, George lost the Republican nomination to Ronald Reagan. However, Reagan chose him to be his vice presidential running mate. The Reagan-Bush team won a strong victory in November 1980.

The Bushes moved into the vice president's home on January 20, 1981. The mansion was built in 1893 and stands on eleven tree-filled acres. They are part of the grounds of the U.S. Naval Observatory, which includes an actual working observatory, an atomic clock, and a map agency on seventy-seven acres. In front of the mansion is a large oak tree that was planted about two hundred years ago. From the tree hangs a swing, a favorite with all the "grands," as Barbara and George call their grandchildren.

The first-floor library is filled with books about and by vice presidents. On the second floor is a cozy family sitting room, which Barbara decorated with family photographs. To show her patriotism, she displayed only paintings done by American artists, just as she had when George was UN ambassador. She borrowed them from several museums.

Each morning, Barbara and George woke up to country music at about six o'clock. They read the newspapers, watched the news, and drank their juice and coffee in bed. They talked about the news and their plans for the day. At seven, George showered, dressed, and left for his office at the White House.

Barbara's days were filled with appointments. In

the eight years that she was "second lady," she hosted 1,192 events at the vice presidential home. These included many luncheons and dinners for foreign diplomats.

Barbara kept very busy with volunteer work, as she has all her adult life. At Christmastime, she visited children hospitalized with cancer. These visits were in honor of Robin. Each Thanksgiving and Christmas, she brought a package of baked goods to the Washington, D.C., Ronald McDonald House. The house provides shelter for families with children who are receiving medical treatment for serious illnesses. She helped prepare and serve food at Martha's Table, a homeless shelter in Washington, D.C. She donated her old clothing to thrift shops, delivering it personally when her schedule permitted.

Whenever Barbara attended the same function as First Lady Nancy Reagan, she took particular care to let

Mrs. Reagan receive the most attention from news reporters. Barbara believed that part of her job as second lady was to support the president and his wife.

Barbara's favorite activity as second lady was serving as president of the Ladies of the Senate, a group of women whose husbands were senators. The women met every Tuesday morning and did volunteer work for organizations such as the Red Cross or Children's Hospital. She formed strong friendships with many of the women, including Marilyn Quayle. Mrs. Quayle's husband, Dan, later became vice president when George Bush was elected president.

When George decided to run for high office, Barbara chose a special project of her own. She was concerned about issues such as drugs, teen pregnancy, AIDS, and homelessness. But she felt society would be better off if more people could read and write, so her cause became literacy, the teaching of reading.

When George was vice president, Barbara participated in about five hundred literacy campaign events.

As the vice president's wife, she went to about five hundred events dealing with literacy. In 1983 she wrote a book called C. *Fred's Story*. C. Fred "told" about his life with the Bush family. Book sales earned $40,000, which Barbara gave to two literacy groups.

C. Fred died on January 20, 1987. Barbara

missed him terribly. George asked his friend Will Farish to help him pick out a new dog for Barbara. Will chose a brown-spotted English springer spaniel. It was love at first sight. Barbara named her Mildred Kerr Bush after one of her closest friends. She was soon nicknamed Millie.

Millie quickly made herself at home with the Bushes. She often followed George to his office, relaxing on the rug as he held important meetings or talked on the telephone. She enjoyed exploring the mansion grounds, where she chased and caught squirrels, rats, and a possum. Barbara and George hit tennis balls for her, which she chased over the lawns and into the flower beds.

Barbara and George traveled widely when he was vice president, visiting with Americans in all fifty states. George often represented the president at meetings and government affairs throughout the world. Barbara went with him to sixty-eight countries and four territories. She traveled more than a million miles, which is about as much as fifty-four times around the world.

After eight years as vice president, George Bush again campaigned to become president of the United States. During the campaign, some reporters made fun of Barbara's white hair and said she looked old enough to be George's mother. Still, she did her best to answer their questions in a friendly but firm manner.

During the campaign, George often relied on Barbara's advice. He had many paid consultants who helped write his speeches and prepare television and radio commercials. But he counted on Barbara to privately give him loving but honest suggestions about his ideas and his speeches.

George Bush was elected president of the United

States on November 8, 1988. He was sworn into office on January 20, 1989, two hundred years after George Washington was inaugurated. Barbara stood at his side, holding the same Bible that was used when George Washington was sworn in as president.

After the inauguration, the Bushes led a parade down Pennsylvania Avenue to the White House. Barbara brought along a pair of low-heeled shoes so that she and George could get out of their car and walk part of the parade route.

Barbara began her life as first lady with her typical enthusiasm. As she gave White House tours to her friends and staff, she pointed out a false wall that hides a secret staircase. Part of the tour was the Lincoln Bedroom. There Abraham Lincoln's only signed copy of the Gettysburg Address is displayed.

From her upstairs office, Barbara can wave to George if he looks up from his desk in the Oval

Office. They made a special point of choosing the Monroe Room as George's home office. It was used as an office by President Franklin Pierce, Barbara's great-great-great-uncle.

When she moved into the White House, Barbara did little redecorating. Nancy Reagan had spent a great deal of money remodeling and purchasing new sets of china. But Barbara refused to criticize Mrs. Reagan. She said that Nancy had left the presidential mansion in "sparkling" condition. However, Barbara did rearrange some of the hair dryers in the beauty shop so that she could store her five dozen family scrapbooks there. This room also became the nursery when Millie's six puppies were born in 1989.

The Bushes enjoy entertaining in the White House. They give many formal state dinners, served in the State Dining Room or outdoors in the Rose Garden. They especially like to serve buffet dinners in the second-floor dining room before they show a movie. Sometimes luncheons or dinners are planned quickly, since George has been known to invite twenty guests over on the spur of the moment.

Barbara also enjoys giving teas in the First Ladies' Garden. In the Children's Garden, the names and hand- and footprints of the White House grandchildren are displayed in bronze plaques. The "grands" like to come here to look at the goldfish in the lily pool. A private garden is next to the Oval Office, where the president likes to read or eat lunch.

When she became first lady, Barbara was determined not to change her life-style. While Nancy Reagan was known for her designer clothing, Barbara Bush sometimes wears her bathrobe to walk Millie on the White House grounds. Barbara refuses to dye her hair, even though some people say it makes her look older. She continues to wear her triple strand of fake

Barbara on the White House lawn with Millie and Ranger, one of Millie's puppies.

pearls, even though some reporters have made fun of them. She laughs about her wrinkles.

Each day Barbara rides her exercise bike or swims a mile in the heated outdoor pool. She swims even if it is snowing. As she swims, she listens to books-on-tape through waterproof earphones. She also tries to play tennis twice a week, with partners such as Sandra Day O'Connor, a U.S. Supreme Court justice.

Barbara's day begins at about five-thirty or six, when she walks Millie around the South Lawn drive. After feeding the dog, Barbara reads the newspapers and drinks coffee and juice in bed with George, as they have done for many years.

Barbara's daily schedule includes answering mail, making personal appearances, and planning state dinners and family luncheons. She works closely with her press secretary, Anna Perez. Perez is the first black woman ever to hold this position.

The first lady's choice points out Barbara's lifelong interest in equal rights for all people. When George was at Yale, Barbara helped him raise money for the United Negro College Fund. In the 1980s, she spent hundreds of hours publicizing and raising money for the medical school at Atlanta's Morehouse College, a black institution. In her work on the Morehouse board, she came to know Dr. Louis Sullivan. She encouraged George to appoint him to his first cabinet as secretary of the Department of Health and Human Services.

As first lady, Barbara continues her work with literacy groups. She serves on the board of Reading Is Fundamental (RIF), a group that gives books to children who have none. In twenty-two years, RIF has given away more than eighty-six million books. In September 1990 she hosted a radio show called "Mrs. Bush's Story Time." During the show's ten programs,

Barbara read aloud selections from children's books.

In March 1989 she formed the Barbara Bush Foundation for Family Literacy. Individuals and large corporations donate money to the foundation. Foundation officials then choose reading programs to receive grant money. The foundation has already given more than half a million dollars to reading programs throughout the United States. Additional funds have come from the sale of *Millie's Book*, the story of the "first dog's" life in the White House.

Barbara calls her volunteer work "giving back." She believes that because her life has been blessed, she should share some of her blessings with others. She knows that volunteers cannot correct every problem in America, but each person can make a difference helping in his or her own neighborhood. She says, "Some people give time, some money, some their skills and connections, some literally give their life's blood . . . but everyone has something to give."

She describes her feelings in a story about a child walking on the beach with his grandfather. The child throws several starfish back into the ocean. The grandfather says, "There are millions of them on the beach; you can't make a difference." The child answers, "Well, I can for this one," and throws another starfish back into the water.

George and Barbara have been happily married for forty-six years.

The Time of Her Life

Barbara Bush says, "The best time of my life is right now." Then she smiles and admits that she would have said the same thing last year and each year before. Her life has had its ups and downs, but she tries to enjoy herself no matter what is going on.

Her husband is a big part of why she enjoys life. "I was lucky the day I met George Bush because he's so good," she recalls. George calls Barbara his mainstay and says he couldn't get along without her, nor could she get along without him.

In their forty-six years of marriage, they have worked out ways to handle problems. When one feels down, the other is encouraging. If they disagree, they discuss the issue right away. Barbara offers

George her opinions in private, but will not disagree with him in public. Whenever they disagreed over family rules, Barbara and George didn't let their children know. They talked about their disagreements in private, so they could face the children with a united front.

Their children recall, though, that Barbara was usually the one who handled discipline. "My dad was hardly around," says Jeb. They remember Barbara for her strong opinions and her ability to tell if they were lying. They nicknamed their mother the "silver fox" because of her white hair, quick mind, and sharp eyesight. Now that all the Bush children are parents themselves, they see the need for the discipline Barbara used when they were growing up. "She'd understand, she'd listen to reason, but somebody had to set the guidelines," Doro recalls.

Barbara is thrilled with her life as first lady. She

and George often share lunches or candlelight dinners. Sunday nights they may tell their cooking staff to go home. Then they have friends in for casual dinners. Sometimes they munch on granola and other snacks or Chinese food from a take-out restaurant. When they go out to eat, they like to go to the Peking Gourmet restaurant in Falls Church, Virginia. Barbara's favorite meal includes Peking duck and orange beef.

Although Barbara loves being first lady, not everything about it is perfect. She admits to having had hurt feelings when reporters said she looked older than her husband. At inauguration time, she came down with Graves' disease. This condition of the thyroid gland causes double vision and swollen eyes. Medication and her sense of humor helped Barbara deal with it. "I'm Popeye the sailor man," she sang cheerily to a news photographer who snapped a picture of her when her eyes were especially bulging.

Her son Neil has been criticized for his actions as a director of a failed savings and loan bank in Colorado. He convinced the bank to loan money to some of his business associates. Bank directors are not supposed to do this. George has been criticized for raising taxes, sending troops to the Persian Gulf, and failing to solve the country's crime and drug problems.

Barbara Bush meets such problems and criticism with intelligence and patience. She fiercely defends her children and refuses to debate her husband's decisions with reporters. "Don't think I don't worry," she said about the Persian Gulf War. "But I can't think of anyone who would do better than George." She also showed support by hanging a yellow wreath from the White House window and visiting military bases to meet with troops' families.

Another way she handles problems and worry is by thinking about the joys of the present. A particular joy is the continuing closeness of her family. She enjoys spending time with George's mother, Dorothy Walker Bush, and admits being closer to the elder Mrs. Bush than she was to her own mother.

The entire family is very close. "We just love our children and they know it," she says. She enjoys spending time with her twelve grandchildren. They come two or three at a time to the White House for movies, fun, and cozy sleep-overs. Sometimes she takes them to museums or the zoo.

The entire Bush clan enjoys getting together each August at the vacation home in Kennebunkport, Maine. The "grands" love to join "Ganny" and "Gampy" in bed in the morning. After a breakfast of pancakes or muffins, everyone goes his or her own way. Some play tennis, softball, horseshoes, or golf,

The Bush grandchildren love to join their grandparents in bed in the morning at Kennebunkport.

while others swim and boat. The younger children enjoy the wonderful collection of toys, such as a fleet of scooters and ride-in toy cars that roar and buzz.

Barbara relaxes in her garden, where she has planted many peonies. She wants them to bloom for the next hundred years, for her children and grandchildren. Other favorite flowers are lilies, gardenias, and daisies. She enjoys prowling nearby antique shops with friends such as Betsy Heminway. She relaxes, reading mysteries and suspense novels. She plays on the beach for hours with the "grands," especially when George meets with important government leaders back at the house.

As "Mrs. President Bush," Barbara is often in the news. This helps her highlight the volunteer causes that she supports. She says that for years, she was only able to donate her time or her money. Now, through television and news stories, she can tell millions of

Barbara relaxes in her garden at Kennebunkport.

people about the needs of others. For example, she has been seen on the news kissing babies with AIDS. Such photographs show that she is not afraid to touch AIDS patients, and encourage others to reach out to help those suffering with AIDS.

Barbara says, "I'm the luckiest woman in the world." On the surface, her job looks easy. She gets to live in a big house, travel a lot, and plan fancy parties. Someone else has to cook and clean up. But in reality, she works hard for no pay. Her children are supposed to be perfect, even though everyone knows that is not really possible. Television and newspaper reporters ask her personal questions. All the while, she must smile and act as if she enjoys every minute.

Yet Barbara Bush seems to be just this sort of person. She enjoys supporting her husband in his career and is happy that she chose to stay home and raise her children. However, she knows that most women today, including her staff and her own daughter, work outside the home. She remains proud of her life choices and believes each woman needs to choose what is best for her family.

Still, she has been criticized for this position. In June 1990, she gave a graduation speech at Wellesley, a women's college. Many of the students were unhappy that Mrs. Bush was selected to be keynote speaker. They felt college officials had chosen her because she was the president's wife, not because of her own successes. Barbara did not get angry with the students who expressed this opinion. Instead, she gently insisted in her speech that families are more important than careers. She said, "At the end of your life . . . you will regret time not spent with a husband, a child, a friend, or a parent."

But she softened her comments with wit. She added that there might be someone in the audience who would follow in her footsteps as the president's spouse. After a pause, she added, "And I wish him well." The audience roared with laughter and applauded.

While all Americans may not agree with Barbara Bush, most seem to respect her for the calm, firm way she states her opinions. Her husband has spoken about the sort of people needed to make a kinder, gentler world. Barbara Bush, with her natural way of putting people at ease, is one of those people. At the end of the 1988 campaign, George Bush predicted that if he won, "America will fall in love with Barbara Bush." She seems to be the right woman in the right place at the right time for the America of the 1990s.

Index

About the Author

Karen Spies is a free-lance writer and part-time ski instructor at Copper Mountain Resort in Colorado. She has written two other Taking Part biographies, *Raffi: The Children's Voice* and *George Bush: Power of the President*. The author has also written articles for many periodicals such as *Writer's Digest, Highlights, Jack and Jill, Children's Digest*, and *Child Life*.

Ms. Spies gives workshops on writing for children, as well as workshops for young writers. She lives with her husband and two children in Littleton, Colorado.